PRiNCE
NOT-SO
CHARMiNG

Prince Not-So Charming

Once Upon a Prank

Her Royal Slyness

The Dork Knight

Happily Ever Laughter

PRINCE NOT-SO CHARMING
Happily Ever Laughter

Roy L. Hinuss
Illustrated by Matt Hunt

[Imprint]
MAKE YOUR MARK

New York

[Imprint]
MAKE YOUR MARK

A part of Macmillan Publishing Group, LLC
175 Fifth Avenue, New York, NY 10010

Library of Congress Control Number: 2018936699

ISBN 978-1-250-14244-3 (paperback) / ISBN 978-1-250-14243-6 (ebook)

Our books may be purchased in bulk for promotional, educational, or
business use. Please contact your local bookseller or the Macmillan
Corporate and Premium Sales Department at (800) 221-7945 ext. 5442 or
by email at MacmillanSpecialMarkets@macmillan.com.

Book design by Ellen Duda

Illustrations by Matt Hunt

Imprint logo designed by Amanda Spielman

First edition, 2018

1   3   5   7   9   10   8   6   4   2

mackids.com

You stole this book? Oh no! Oh geez!
You must return it! Hurry! Please!
If you do not, you'll rue the day
The Dreaded Book Curse came your way!
Your nails will crack. Your tongue will numb.
You'll crush eight fingers and one thumb.
Your knees will bruise. Your pants will tear.
Your nose will sprout a four-foot hair.
You'll get a cut that just won't heal.
You'll find dead flies in every meal.
Your life will stink without a break!
So BUY this book, for heaven's sake!

To Lord John,

royal scribe and donkey whisperer

CHAPTER 1

Prince Carlos Charles Charming raced down the twisty corridors of Fancy Castle. He'd been told to get to the throne room "on the double."

"On the double" didn't mean "in a minute." "On the double" meant "*now*."

Carlos's dad, King Carmine, didn't say

"on the double" very often. When he did, it usually meant bad news. Carlos quickened his pace. His jingle-toed shoes slapped against the castle floors. His stomach knotted up with worry.

Carlos wasn't only worried; he was crabby, too. His dad's "on the double" had arrived in the middle of Carlos's jester lesson.

What could possibly be more important than jestering? Carlos's brain grouched as he skidded around another corner. *Why don't I get an "on the double" when I'm doing something princely?*

And why, he wondered as he gasped for breath, *is this castle so dang huge?*

Carlos stumbled through the throne room's arched doorway. King Carmine and Queen Cora were waiting for him.

Carlos's parents were a study in opposites: His dad was tall and thin. His mom was short and plump. His dad was a serious man of few words. His mom was a giggly chatterbox.

At least, his mom was *usually* a giggly chatterbox. As Carlos staggered toward the thrones, he noticed that she was not her usual self. For the first time in forever, she shared her husband's frown. Also for the first time in forever, she allowed her husband to do most of the talking.

"Ah, there you are, son," the king said. "Thank you for coming so quickly. We have a visitor."

It was then that Carlos noticed the stranger. He was large and round and sickly pale. (He looked *especially* sickly standing beside the tan-skinned king and queen.) The stranger's head seemed to ooze into his torso like a dollop of whipped yolk sitting in a deviled egg. His uniform was black silk trimmed with gold. His most prominent feature, however, was his nose. It was as long and sharp as a toucan's beak. It pointed straight up, showing off what Carlos imagined were the hairiest nostrils on earth.

Ew, Carlos thought.

"This man is a special messenger from Dire Dominion," the king said.

Carlos knew of Dire Dominion. It was a vast land, seven or eight kingdoms to the west of Faraway Kingdom. The dominion was famous for its huge and powerful army that always seemed to be waging war on somebody.

The messenger looked down his nose at Carlos. His nasal hair flapped with disapproval. "This," he sneered, "is a *prince*?"

Carlos peered down at his clothes. He was wearing a lime-green jester suit, complete with hat and curly-toed shoes. It was a snappy outfit but not a very princely one.

"Yes," the king replied, clenching his jaw. "He is the prince. A very *excellent* prince, I might add. So give us your message and go."

Carlos noticed that his dad wasn't quite himself. King Carmine was usually calm and patient with everyone, but now anger lurked behind his every word. It was unsettling. A twinge of anxiety caught in Carlos's throat.

"The message is not to be *given*," the messenger intoned. "It is to be *announced*. It is to be read aloud by me."

"Of course it is." The king's eyes narrowed. "I would expect nothing less from Queen Cayenne. Read your message and get out."

The messenger reached into the large, black leather satchel draped over his shoulder.

He pulled out a trumpet.

He took a deep breath, puckered, and blew.

Triumphant fanfare echoed off the walls and ceiling of the throne room.

The king let out a sharp, impatient sigh.

The messenger returned the trumpet to the satchel.

He then pulled out a drum.

Thunderous booms echoed off the walls and ceiling of the throne room.

The king let out a second sharp, impatient sigh.

The messenger returned the drum to his satchel.

He then pulled out a—

"If you pull another instrument out of that bag," the king said, "I will have you stabbed."

"Queen Cayenne ordered me to play five instruments," the messenger replied.

"*Five* instruments?" The king turned to Carlos. "Son? Will you fetch my sword?"

"All right! All right!" the messenger shouted. "I'll read the message!"

The messenger reached back into his bag. He nudged past an accordion, banjo, and tambourine and pulled out a scroll tied with a ribbon.

The messenger unrolled the crinkly document. He cleared his throat. Then he read:

"'The brave, noble, and super-duper kingdom of Dire Dominion, wisely ruled by the courageous, compassionate, and super-

gorgeous Queen Cayenne, is proud, honored, and super-stoked to announce the 10 and ¾th birthday of the scholarly, athletic, and super-popular Prince Hortense.

"'To celebrate this awesome-sauce occa- sion, one prince or princess from every kingdom on the continent will attend Prince Hortense's 10 and ¾th birthday party, to be held in Dominion Palace on the first of June at three o'clock.

"'If your prince or princess does not attend Prince Hortense's 10 and ¾th birthday party, Dire Dominion will see this insult as an act of war.'"

A jolt of fear zipped up Carlos's spine.

"'If your prince or princess is late to Prince Hortense's 10 and ¾th birthday party, Dire Dominion will see this insult as an act of war.'"

Carlos's head began to pound.

"'If your prince or princess is not dressed

in his or her finest clothing for Prince Hortense's 10 and ¾th birthday party, Dire Dominion will see this insult as an act of war.'"

Carlos's legs got wobbly.

"'If your prince or princess does not arrive with an expensive and thoughtful gift for Prince Hortense's 10 and ¾th birthday party, Dire Dominion will see this insult as an act of war.'"

Carlos felt like he was about to throw up.

"'In short, if your prince or princess does anything—and we mean anything—that we don't like, Dire Dominion is gonna wipe your piddly kingdom off the face of the earth.

"'Can't wait to see you there!

"'Signed Queen Cayenne, Absolute Ruler of Dire Dominion, the Catapult Capital of the World.'"

The messenger rolled up the scroll and strode from the room.

"This is going to be a fart stink of a party," Carlos said.

"Don't say 'fart stink.' It's unprincely," the king replied. "But yes. It will be."

"Oh, how I hate that Queen Cayenne!" Queen Cora snapped. "She is so very, very . . ."

"Fart stinky?" Carlos suggested.

"Yes! Fart stinky! Very fart stinky!" She turned to the king. "That sister of yours is always looking for a way to make your life difficult."

Carlos's mouth dropped open in surprise. "Wait, what? Dad has a sister?!"

The king nodded. "Queen Cayenne is my younger sister."

"Really? How come I've never heard of her?" Carlos asked. "How come she doesn't show up on holidays? Or come to family gatherings? Or send me birthday cards with money inside?"

"We, um, prefer not to speak about her too much," the king said.

Queen Cora put it a little more bluntly. "Because Queen Cayenne is the most terrible, horrible, no good, very bad person on the continent. And I get along with *everybody*! But whenever I hear from that fartstinky sister of your father's, I just want to . . . I just want to . . . I . . . I . . ." she sputtered. "Oh! I don't even know what I want!"

The king rose from his chair. "That's all right, dear. *I* know what you want." He called to a nearby servant. "Fetch the dragon, please. Her Majesty needs something to cuddle."

"Ooh! Yes!" A smile stretched across Queen Cora's face. "That is *exactly* what I want! A good dragon cuddle!"

"I know, dear," the king replied.

"You always look out for me," she continued.

"That's my job." The king kissed her forehead. "And don't worry about Cayenne. She likes to cause trouble sometimes, but I know my sister. Everything is going to turn out just fine."

The king's words sounded reassuring, but Carlos saw something the queen did not. Carlos saw a flicker of worry in his father's eyes. Carlos had never seen his father worried before.

Never.

Carlos felt himself go numb. *This is bad,* he thought. *This is very, very bad.*

CHAPTER 2

"Ah, there you are, young'un!" Jack the Jester said in surprise. "I wasn't sure if you were coming back."

Carlos leaned heavily against the doorway of Fancy Castle's ballroom. "I wasn't sure, either," Carlos said.

"No worries," the old jester said. "Now, if I remember correctly, you were going to show me a new juggling routine."

"Yeah," Carlos replied. His mind was a million miles away.

If I do anything wrong at that party, I could start a war, Carlos thought.

"All right, then," Jack said. "Dazzle me!"

Jack handed Carlos three plastic sporks. Carlos accepted them.

One little itty-bitty mistake and I could start a war! Carlos thought.

Jack tapped his jingle-toed shoe. "Well, come on, kiddo! Do something! Don't keep me in suspense! I assume your routine has something to do with that cake?"

Jack gestured to the far side of the ballroom, where three perfect slices of cake rested on a pedestal.

The word *cake* snapped Carlos out of his troubled trance.

"Hmm? Oh, yeah. The cake," he began. "I'll be jestering for the Stein triplets next

week. It's their birthday. So I came up with a new idea: I'll juggle these three sporks. At the end of my juggling routine, I'll throw them at three slices of birthday cake. One spork will stick into each slice. That way the triplets can eat their cake the second I'm finished performing."

"Wow! That sounds amazing!" Jack exclaimed. "*If* you can do it."

Jack said "If you can do it" with a twinkle in his eye. Jack was *sure* Carlos could do it. Carlos was probably the best juggler on the continent.

And Carlos *could* do it. Carlos had practiced this spork routine hundreds of times

21

on hundreds of cake slices. Every time he practiced, the result was always the same: Each spork neatly plopped tines-first into the buttercream icing.

But as Carlos began to juggle the sporks, his mind once again swelled with troubling thoughts.

He tried to push the thoughts away.

Don't think about starting a war. Don't think about starting a war. Don't think about starting a war, Carlos thought.

But that didn't work.

He tried to focus.

Focus! Carlos thought. *Focus on the juggling. Focus on the exact spots where you want the sporks to land. Not on starting a war. Don't focus on starting a war!*

But that didn't work, either.

Holy schmoley! Carlos thought. *I could start a war!*

And Carlos threw the sporks.

This is what happened next:

1. The first spork missed the cake. Instead, it crashed through a colorful stained-glass window.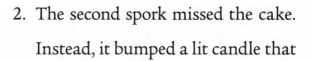

2. The second spork missed the cake. Instead, it bumped a lit candle that

set fire to a rope that held up a crystal chandelier. The chandelier crashed to the ballroom floor.

3. The third spork missed the cake. Instead, it stabbed an oil painting. The oil painting was of Cornelius, the royal horse. The spork stabbed the painting of the royal horse in the painting's royal horsey butt.

Jack and Carlos regarded the destruction for a long, silent moment. Carlos had no idea plastic sporks could create so much mayhem. But apparently they can.

"Maybe I'm wrong, kiddo," Jack said, "but you seem a little distracted."

"I am distracted!" Carlos exclaimed. "I'm *really* distracted! I just got a message from a fart-stinky queen from some fart-stinky country! She invited me to a fart-stinky birthday party for a fart-stinky kid I don't even know! And there are, like, three million fart-stinky rules I have to follow! And if I mess up any fart-stinky rule, this fart-stinky queen from this fart-stinky country will wage a war on Faraway Kingdom!" Carlos gasped for breath. "It's just so . . ."

"Fart stinky?" Jack asked. The kindly old jester scratched his chin. "Is the name of the country Dire Dominion?"

Carlos's eyebrows went up in surprise. "Yeah," he said.

"And is the queen named Cayenne?" Jack asked.

"How did you know that?" Carlos asked.

"I know Cayenne," Jack said. "Or I *knew* her. When she was a little girl, she used to live in this castle with your father. I jestered for her."

"Oh, of course," Carlos said.

"And you know what?" Jack asked.

"What?" Carlos asked.

"She was always rotten," Jack said.

Minutes later, Carlos and Jack stood in the hall outside the king's study. They stared at a life-size painting of a scowling, bony woman. She held a rat-size, scowling, bony dog in her lap.

"That's Cayenne," Jack said. "Never in all my years did I ever catch that girl smiling. Your father didn't smile much, either. But your father was different. King Carmine was serious but *happy*." Jack shook his head sadly. "But Cayenne was *never* happy. Never. Not once. And she was jealous of anyone who was."

Carlos stared into Cayenne's face. The angry glint in her eyes gave him chills.

"Cayenne *hated* happy people. That's why she hates your father," Jack said.

Carlos shuddered at the idea. "I didn't know family members could be like that. I mean, I know families argue, but to actually *hate* one another?"

"That hatred is common in many families. Especially royal families," Jack said. "And Cayenne has hate to spare. That's why I come here to practice my aim."

"Practice your aim?" Carlos asked.

"Yep." A jet of water fired from the flower on Jack's lapel. The stream caught the scowling Cayenne right between the eyes. A second squirt hit the scowling rat dog.

Jack smiled. "Dang, I'm good."

"But I don't understand," Carlos said. "If Cayenne is such a horrible person, why is there a picture of her hanging outside Dad's study?"

"It's a reminder," came the reply. But the reply was not from Jack.

Carlos turned. The door to the study was open. King Carmine took a step into the hall. "That portrait helps me rule this kingdom," he said. "When I am faced with a difficult decision, I ask myself, 'What would Cayenne do?' Then I do the opposite."

Jack bowed before the king. "I hope I wasn't getting too personal, Your Majesty."

The king shook his head. "Not at all, Jack. It's important for Carlos to know about my sister." The king turned to Carlos. "Tomorrow is Hortense's party. You will be wandering into a lion's den."

"I know," Carlos said.

"My sister will look for any excuse to wage war on Faraway Kingdom," the king said. "Do your best to not give her that excuse."

Carlos's throat tightened. "I'm scared." His voice was little more than a squeak. "I'm scared that I might drop my salad spork and start a war."

"I know how you feel." The king put his hand on Carlos's shoulder. "But I *also* know something else. I know that you are a very capable, intelligent, and resourceful prince."

The king gave Jack a respectful nod. "And thanks to my old friend Jack, you are *also* a

very capable, intelligent, and resourceful *jester.* Those qualities have served you very well in the past. I have a feeling they will serve you well tomorrow."

But Carlos wasn't so sure.

CHAPTER 3

Carlos stood outside the castle, waiting for his ride.

He wore his white suit. It was his finest suit. It also happened to be his most uncomfortable suit. The starched collar squeezed his neck. The heavy jacket pinched his shoulders. The stiff belt dug into his stomach. The handle of his sword poked his thigh. The slightly too-small trousers made his butt itchy. The shiny boots pinched his pinkie toe.

Every inch of him was scrubbed raw. His fingernails were clipped. His teeth were flossed. His tangle of hair was combed within an inch of its life.

Carlos was so miserable that he barely noticed the thunder of approaching footsteps.

"Oh, hai, CC!" Smudge chirped.

Smudge was Carlos's ride. Smudge was also Fancy Castle's dragon. Castles don't typically have dragons, but Smudge was not a typical dragon. He was the size of a teenaged bull elephant but had the happy personality of a guinea pig in a barrel of baby carrots. Smudge worked at the castle lighting chandeliers with his fiery breath, giving knitting lessons, and accepting snuggles from Queen Cora.

Smudge inspected Carlos from head to toe. "Ooh! CC! You look snappy!"

"I don't feel snappy," Carlos grouched. His collar squeezed him tighter and tighter. "I feel achy. All over. Even my hair hurts."

"Well, I think you're snappy from head to bootstrap-y!" Smudge could always be counted on to be enthusiastic. "Hop on and we'll get going."

Carlos did as he was told. First, he belted to the dragon's back a saddle made from pink yarn. It was one of Smudge's knitting projects.

Then he stuffed Hortense's birthday present into the saddlebag and climbed onto Smudge's back.

"This day is going to be awful," Carlos grumbled.

"No, it won't," Smudge said.

"Yes, it will," Carlos replied.

"No, it won't, CC," Smudge said. "Do you know why?"

Carlos struggled with his collar button. It wouldn't budge. "Why?"

"Because we're bestest buddies!" Smudge put a little bounce in his walk. "And we're together! And that is the bestest thing ever!"

"Well, that's true," Carlos admitted.

"Aaaaand," Smudge continued, "we're going to pick up our other bestest buddy, Pinky! So we'll soon be *three* bestest buddies!

Three bestest buddies being bestest buddies together!

"And that is the bestest!" Smudge added.

"Yeah," Carlos admitted again.

Pinky was the princess of Ever-After Land. She was being forced to go to Dire Dominion, too.

If anyone can help me get through this fart-stinky party, it'll be Pinky, Carlos thought.

Carlos's mood improved a little.

Then, with a grunt, he finally unfastened his collar button. He could breathe again.

His mood improved a little more.

Now that the collar didn't distract him so much, Carlos noticed other things. He found a small bulge in the breast pocket of his jacket. He reached inside to see what it was.

"Huh," Carlos mused. "How did my hand buzzer get in here?"

"I put it there," Smudge replied.

"Why?"

Smudge made a little "pfft" noise, as if the answer was super-obvious. "Because it's *fun*!" the dragon announced. "You're going

to a party, right? Parties are supposed to be fun!"

A few minutes later, Smudge trotted past Faraway Kingdom's royal barn. The barn doors were lying on the ground. They had been knocked from their hinges.

"What happed over there?" Carlos asked.

"Oh, didn't ya hear?" Smudge said. "The royal horse escaped last night."

Carlos gasped so sharply that he sucked in a dragonfly. "What?!" he sputtered, hacking up bug guts. "Cornelius escaped? Have they found him? Do they know here he is?"

"No, but don't worry. They say he's lurking nearby," Smudge said with a nod.

"Cornelius is *lurking nearby*?" Carlos's eyes darted from one possible hiding spot to another. "He's waiting for me! He wants to get me! You know how much it hurts when you stub your toe?"

"Uh-huh." Smudge nodded.

"Well, Cornelius wants to stub my *whole body*!"

"Cornelius wants to whole-body stub you?" Smudge asked. "What for?"

"What for?!" Carlos exclaimed. "We've talked about this a million times! That horse hates me!"

"Why? Because of that time you hand-buzzered his butt?" Smudge asked.

"Yes," Carlos answered.

"But that was only a little prank," Smudge replied.

"But then there was—" Carlos began.

"The time you threw an acorn at his butt?" Smudge asked.

"Yes," Carlos said.

"But that was to rescue me," Smudge replied.

"But don't forget—" Carlos began.

"The time you kicked a rock and it hit his butt?" Smudge asked.

"Yes!" Carlos nearly shouted.

"But that was an accident," Smudge replied.

"But then there was—" Carlos began.

"The time I set fire to his butt?" Smudge asked.

"YES!" Carlos shouted.

"But that wasn't even *you*," Smudge replied. "*I* burned Cornelius's butt with *my* hot bref."

"Yes, I know," Carlos said. "But you burned him because I startled you. Cornelius blames *me* for that."

A leaf crinkled somewhere beyond the trees. Carlos flinched. "That horse is just waiting for the right time to get me. And when he gets me, he's going to whole-body stub me."

"Don't worry, CC!" Smudge said. "I won't let nobody whole-body stub you. That's what bestest buddies are for. To keep their bestest buddy's body from getting the stubbin's. That's just common sense."

That made Carlos feel a little better, but only a little.

As Smudge trotted on toward Ever-After Land, Carlos kept scanning the trees, searching for any sign of a vengeful horse.

CHAPTER 4

Carlos began to breathe more easily once they crossed into Ever-After Land. It was easy to relax here. The kingdom was as pretty as one of Pinky's oil paintings. Everywhere he looked, he saw vibrant greenery waving in the gentle breeze.

Carlos was *also* relaxed because, unlike the thick forests of Faraway Kingdom, Ever-After Land was made up of farms. Long, straight rows of vegetables stretched to the horizon.

I'm safe from Cornelius now, Carlos thought. *A horse can't hide behind a carrot stalk.*

Minutes later, they arrived at Ever-After Castle. Pinky stood on the edge of the draw-bridge, looking miserable. She was wedged into a shining pink gown. Her ebony skin glowed. Her black hair, braided, pinned, and piled impossibly high, was topped with a pink tiara. On her feet were pink glass shoes.

Carlos's mouth dropped open. This was the first time he had ever seen Pinky wearing anything besides paint-spattered overalls.

"Wow" was all he could say.

Smudge, on the other hand, had plenty to say. "Oh, Pinky! That dress! Those shoes! That tiara! You look like a starry night! A twinkly holiday! A chandelier with every candle aglow!"

"Thanks," Pinky replied. She pulled herself into the saddle behind Carlos. She dumped a small, wrapped present into the saddlebag.

Carlos cleared his throat. "You, um, *do* look very nice," he told her. "I mean, you *always* look nice. But you also look nice like this."

"Thanks," Pinky said again. "But I hate everything about this outfit. Especially the shoes. Whoever came up with the idea of glass shoes? My feet are killing me. And what if they break? It's like walking on danger!"

"Walking on danger?" Carlos asked.

"Hey, I can't think straight when my feet hurt!" Pinky grouched. Then she groaned. "Okay. Let's get this fart-stinky thing over with."

"Okeydokey!" Smudge exclaimed as he skipped down the country path. "Yay! Three bestest buddies together at last! Next stop, Dire Dominion!"

◆ ◆ ◆

Smudge was true to his word. He paused only once on the long journey: He needed to know what a dandelion smelled like.

The dragon frowned. "It doesn't smell like anything," he sighed. "There should be a law against flowers not smelling like anything."

"A law?" Carlos couldn't help but smile.

"Yuh-huh." Smudge nodded. "Someone should spray these flowers so they smell like something nice. Like bacon, or chocolate. Or chocolate bacon."

"Or flowers?" Pinky asked.

"I guess." Smudge shrugged. "But I'd prefer my flowers to smell like chocolate bacon."

◆ ◆ ◆

They continued on, through tunnels and over bridges, across fields and down twisty roads. The views were beautiful.

Then, all of a sudden, the views *stopped* being beautiful.

The land grew dusty and rocky. The trees were cut down. Carlos, Pinky, and Smudge found themselves trudging through a depressing field of spongy, rotten stumps.

Everything is brown and gray, Carlos thought. He looked up to the clouds. *Even the sky is brown and gray.*

"We must be close," Pinky muttered.

"Yup," Smudge said. "There it is."

Dire Dominion's outer wall loomed in

the distance. It stretched from one end of the horizon to the other and was made up of nothing but tree trunks. The trunks were sunk into the ground. They were tied together so tightly that no daylight could shine between them.

The wall was at least thirty feet high. Maybe higher. It encircled the entire dominion.

"Look at that," Pinky said. "They must've killed a hundred thousand trees to make that wall."

"Probably more," Carlos said. "The dominion is pretty big."

"What a waste! They destroyed a whole forest to make that ugly thing!" She was furious now. Pinky liked to paint land-scapes. In her view, nothing was more beau-tiful than a forest.

"YOU THERE! DON'T MOVE!" a voice bellowed. It came from the other side of the wall.

The main gate groaned open. A soldier with the broad shoulders of a gorilla emerged. He was dressed in animal fur. Or maybe he was just a very hairy person. Carlos wasn't sure.

A sword hung from the soldier's belt. Also on his belt were half a dozen daggers, a mace, and an ax. The soldier held a crossbow, which he pointed at Smudge's head.

"Oh . . . um . . . hai." Smudge gulped.

"Dragons aren't allowed in Dire Domin-ion," the soldier growled. "They are to be killed on sight."

He took careful aim.

"Wait!" Carlos shouted. "You can't do that! We're guests of Queen Cayenne!"

"Those are Queen Cayenne's orders," the soldier said. "Her husband, the great King Hubert, was killed by a dragon. So we are commanded to kill any and all dragons in the dominion."

"But we're not *in* the dominion!" Carlos said.

"You're *near* the dominion," the soldier said. "You're headed *toward* the dominion."

"*Near* is not the same as *in*!" Pinky said. She leapt from Smudge's back and strode toward the soldier with great purpose. "Did the queen say kill all dragons *in* the dominion or kill all dragons *near* the dominion?"

The soldier wavered for a moment. "In," he said. "In the dominion."

"Are we *in* the dominion?" Pinky asked.

"No," he admitted.

"We aren't in the dominion, but you were going to kill the dragon anyway!" Pinky poked a manicured finger into the soldier's furry chest. "Do you know how much trouble you are in right now?"

"I'm not in trouble!" the soldier protested, suddenly nervous.

"Oh, you're not?" Pinky gave the man another poke. "You were going to kill our dragon *outside* the dominion. Even though Queen Cayenne *told* you to kill dragons *inside* the dominion! You are disobeying the queen!"

"No, I wasn't," the soldier cried. "Not really!"

"Disobeying the queen is a crime! You are

committing a crime!" Pinky shouted this for all the world to hear. "And I have *a witness*."

Carlos's ears perked up. This was his cue to speak. "That's right," he said. "I'm a witness."

"And me, too! I'm a witness, too!" Smudge bounced a little. "I've always wanted to be a witness. And now I am!"

"Two witnesses," Pinky said. "Boy, I wouldn't want to be in your shoes. And *my* shoes are made of *glass*. Do you know why most shoes aren't made of glass? Hmm? Because glass *hurts*, man! It hurts *bad*! And yet I *still* prefer my shoes to yours! *That's* how much trouble you're in!"

"All right!" the soldier shouted. "I won't kill the dragon!"

"I know you won't." Pinky delivered another poke.

"But that dragon ain't coming inside this wall!" he shouted. "You two are going to walk from here!"

"Fine," Pinky said with a poke.

"AND STOP POKING ME!" the soldier shouted.

"Where's the castle?" Pinky asked.

"A mile that way!" he snarled.

Pinky looked uneasily at her aching feet. "A . . . *mile*?"

Carlos slid off of Smudge's back. "Sorry you can't go any farther, buddy," he said, petting the dragon's snout. "It's for your own safety."

"That's okay, CC." Smudge propped himself against an especially large tree stump. He pulled out his knitting bag. "I'll keep myself busy."

◆ ◆ ◆

Carlos and Pinky walked down the streets of Dire Dominion.

There was nothing but weapons as far as

the eye could see. Catapults, siege towers, and battering rams. Swords, clubs, and pikes. Carlos had never seen so many weapons in one place before.

"Where are the houses?" Carlos whispered. "There aren't any houses."

"People live inside the cannons," Pinky whispered back.

"What? That can't be true," Carlos replied.

"Oh, it's true all right!" someone said.

Carlos and Pinky turned to the sound of the voice. They found a smiling granny poking her head out of the barrel of a nearby cannon. "Oh, aren't you two dressed beautifully! Would you like to come in for a snack? My crumb cake is almost ready."

"Oh. No, thank you," Carlos replied. "Wait, what? You have a kitchen in there?"

"Of course! Come on in. I'll just set a couple of extra places in the formal dining room."

"You have a formal dining room in there, too?" Carlos asked.

"Oh, yes. And a game room with an air hockey table! It's a *very* big cannon," the woman replied cheerily. "I live here quite comfortably when we're not waging war. And

when we *are* waging war, my house destroys

kingdoms! Isn't that wonderful?"

Actually, it didn't sound very wonderful

at all.

Don't forget to be perfect, Carlos told him-

self. *Faraway Kingdom's survival depends on it.*

CHAPTER 5

"This is it," Carlos said, taking a deep breath.

"Yeah," Pinky replied.

They stared at the giant door of Dominion Palace.

"We should knock," Carlos said.

"Yeah," Pinky replied.

But both of them just stood there.

"We should really . . ." Carlos trailed off.

"Yeah," Pinky replied.

"All right," Carlos sighed. "I'll knock."

But he never got the chance. Without warning, the door flew open.

Queen Cayenne towered over them.

She looked almost exactly like the portrait that hung outside King Carmine's study. She was a little older and her skin was stretched a little tighter against a slightly bonier face, but otherwise, she didn't look different at all.

Well, *one* thing was different. Instead of a scowl, Queen Cayenne wore a smile. It was not a warm smile or a kind smile but something cheerfully cruel. It was the smile of a cat about to swallow a wounded mouse.

"Well, well, well!" The queen's smile stretched wider, revealing a mouthful of pearly, sharp teeth. "Look who's here! Princess Pinky of Ever-After Land and my dear, dear nephew, Prince Carlos Charles Charming of Faraway Kingdom!"

"Good afternoon, Queen Cayenne," Carlos and Pinky mumbled.

"I have a question for both of you," she said. "Do either of you know how to tell time?"

It was one of those questions that you're not supposed to answer.

The queen snapped her fingers. In an

instant, a prune-faced servant dressed in black was at her elbow.

"Meadows," she said to the servant. "Would you be so kind as to tell these children what time it is?"

"Yes, Your Majesty," Meadows replied. "It is ten minutes after three o'clock."

"Oh, dear." The queen tut-tutted. "That is *late*. Isn't that late, Meadows?"

"Quite late, Your Majesty," Meadows replied.

"Make a note, Meadows," she said. "The prince and princess are *late*."

Meadows flipped open a notebook, plucked a pencil from his breast pocket, and began to write.

"Sorry," Carlos said. "Pinky and I are really sorry."

But Pinky wasn't sorry. "The reason we're

73

late," she said firmly, "is because the guy at the front gate made us walk."

"That is a shame," the queen replied. "But late is *late*."

And the queen was just getting started. "Meadows, please *also* note that Prince Carlos's collar is *unbuttoned*. His shoes are *scuffed*. And his pants cuffs are *muddy*."

"That's because your *streets* are muddy." Pinky's tone wasn't exactly hostile, but it was getting there.

The queen peered down at Pinky's feet. Her eyebrows shot up in surprise. "Where on earth are your shoes?"

Now Pinky was hostile. "I threw them away. Have you ever tried to walk a mile? In the mud? In glass shoes?"

The queen turned to Meadows. "Please *also* note that Princess Pinky decided to visit us dressed as a hobo."

Pinky was going to respond, but Carlos beat her to it. "We're sorry!" Carlos exclaimed. "*Very* sorry! We are both very, very sorry."

"I'm sure you are," the queen replied. "And if you aren't, you *will* be. You may now give me Prince Hortense's birthday presents."

Carlos and Pinky exchanged glances.

"You *do* have presents, don't you?"

"Yes," Carlos said. "Expensive and thoughtful ones. It's just . . ."

The queen's bony hand clamped on to Carlos's lapel. She yanked him forward until they were nose-to-nose. "It's just what?" she growled.

"We accidentally left the presents with Smudge," Carlos squeaked. "When the guard told us to walk to the castle, we forgot to . . ."

"You left them with . . . ?"

"Smudge." Carlos's throat suddenly got very dry.

The queen tightened her grip. For an old, skinny, bony lady, she was pretty strong.

"What is a *smudge*?" she asked.

Don't say dragon, Carlos thought. *The queen hates dragons!*

"Smudge is . . ." Carlos began.

"Smudge is what?" The queen's eyes seemed to grow more fiery by the moment.

Don't say dragon, don't say dragon, don't say dragon! Carlos thought.

But Carlos's brain could only come up with one word. And that word was *dragon*.

"Smudge is a . . ." he tried again.

"HORSE!" Pinky shouted. "We left the gifts with our horse!"

"Yes." Carlos nodded. "Smudge is the name of our horse."

"Do you want us to go back and get the presents?" Pinky asked. "From the horse?"

But Queen Cayenne ignored Pinky's question.

"Let me get this straight," the queen began. "You come to my home late. You dress like hoboes. You do not bring gifts. And, before you even walk through my front door, you attempt to leave. Is that correct?"

"Sort of," Carlos said weakly.

"Meadows, please note every one of these transgressions," the queen commanded.

"I have already noted them, Your Majesty," Meadows said.

"Then note them *again*," she said.

"Yes, Your Majesty." Meadows scribbled notes as fast as the tip of his pencil would allow.

"Well, my dear nephew." The queen's wicked smile returned with a vengeance. "Your first impression is not very impressive. Not. Impressive. At all."

CHAPTER 6

Carlos and Pinky were led to the Dominion
Palace ballroom. Just like everything else in
Dire Dominion, the ballroom was gray and

brown. Even the four enormous stained-glass windows that lined the far wall were made from gray and brown glass. At first Carlos thought the windows might have been dirty. But no. The gray and brown glass glittered and sparkled like polished dirt.

"Well, isn't that pleasant," Pinky mumbled.

The ballroom dance floor was as large as a soccer field, with about three dozen dancers on it. The dancers were young princes and princesses from other kingdoms. All of them looked miserable.

Off in a far corner, a string quartet played a waltz, but it was hard to hear the whispery notes.

It was much easier to hear the burly guard at the front of the room. He stood on an elevated platform and yelled at the dancers below.

"FORWARD! SIDE! TOGETHER!" he yelled. "BACKWARD! SIDE! TOGETHER!"

A second guard with scars running up and down his face stood before a dance chart filled with footprints and arrows. When Burly Guard yelled a command, Scarred Guard used his sword as a pointer. He smacked the blade against the correct foot position on the chart. The dancers then

obediently stomped their feet into that position.

So it was kind of like this:

"FORWARD!" shouted Burly Guard.

SMACK! went the sword.

STOMP! went the dancers' feet.

"SIDE!" shouted Burly Guard.

SMACK! went the sword.

STOMP! went the dancers' feet.

Carlos barely noticed. His mind was too troubled.

Queen Cayenne is going to destroy Faraway Kingdom because of me, he thought. *Dire Dominion is going to destroy everything I love!*

Pinky shook Carlos's shoulder. "Come

on," she said. "The queen says everybody has to dance."

Carlos's eyes turned to the dance floor. He watched the young princes and princesses cling to one another, stomping in unison.

"This is a dance?" Carlos whispered.

Pinky nodded. "The box step. The most boring dance in the world. Come on."

She pulled Carlos to one of the many empty spots on the floor. "Give me your left hand."

"What?" Carlos was still distracted.

So Pinky grabbed Carlos's left hand with her right.

Carlos wasn't distracted anymore. He had never held a girl's hand before.

"Put your other hand on my waist," Pinky said.

"On your . . . ?" Carlos could feel his face get red.

"Yes. My waist," Pinky replied. She grabbed his right hand with her left and placed it where it belonged. "This is called *dancing*. Wake up."

Pinky placed her left hand on his shoulder.

Carlos looked into

Pinky's eyes. "What do I do now?" he asked.

"Listen to the guy who's yelling at us," Pinky replied. "Start with your left foot."

"FORWARD!" shouted Burly Guard.

Carlos moved his left foot forward. At the same time, Pinky expertly moved her right foot back.

"SIDE!" shouted Burly Guard.

Carlos moved his right foot to the side. Pinky moved her left foot to the side.

"TOGETHER!" shouted Burly Guard.

Carlos had to peek at the chart for that one. Then he slid his left foot toward his right. Pinky moved her right foot toward her left.

"Good," Pinky said. "Now do it back
ward, starting with your right foot."

On Burly Guard's "BACKWARD!" Carlos
stepped backward. On "SIDE!" Carlos moved
his left foot to the side. On "TOGETHER!"
Carlos slid his right foot toward his left.

"There you go!" Pinky exclaimed. "You
did the box step!"

"That's it?" Carlos asked.

"That's all." She smiled. "Now keep doing it."

Carlos smiled, too. The box step was kind
of a boring dance, but dancing a boring
dance with Pinky was kind of fun.

Before he could enjoy himself too much,

however, Carlos began to worry again. His smile faded away.

"What's wrong?" Pinky asked.

"I feel horrible," Carlos replied. "Dire Dominion is going to destroy Faraway Kingdom."

"You don't know that," she said.

"Yes, I do. I've already messed up so much," he sighed. "Being late. The unbuttoned collar. The mud. The scuffs. The presents . . ."

"We can't give up," Pinky said. "We just need to look at our problem in a different way."

"What do you mean by 'a different way'?" Carlos asked.

"Look over there." Pinky jerked her head toward the elevated platform. Prince Hortense, rail-thin and sleepy-eyed, was slumped on a golden throne. He watched over the activity below with frowny disinterest. He stuffed mini donuts into his mouth two at a time.

"He doesn't look happy," Carlos said.

"Why *would* he be happy?" Pinky replied. "The only thing more boring than *doing* the box step is *watching other people* do the box step. But maybe . . ."

Carlos continued her thought: "Maybe if we dance a different way . . ."

Pinky finished Carlos's thought: "We'll be the life of the party."

Carlos was suddenly hopeful. "Maybe everyone will be so impressed with our dancing that Dire Dominion won't go to war with us! That's a great idea!"

"Do you know an impressive dance?" Pinky asked.

"Pfft. I'm a jester," Carlos replied. "I probably know more impressive dances than you do."

Pinky put her hands on her hips. "Oh, is this a throwdown?" she asked. "A dance off? Is that what you want?"

Carlos thought for a second. "Yes. That's what I want."

"Bring it," Pinky said.

"I'll start with a simple move," Carlos said. "The Lawn Mower."

With dramatic flair, Carlos crouched on the dance floor. He rhythmically yanked an imaginary pull cord for an imaginary lawn mower. After getting the imaginary lawn mower started, he grabbed its imaginary handle and strutted in a circle.

"That was good," Pinky admitted. "But not good enough. I call *this* move the Get a Mop on That Floor."

"Dazzle me," Carlos said.

Pinky wrung out an imaginary mop in an imaginary bucket. Then, using a two-handed pushing motion, she swayed her hips as she pushed the imaginary mop across the floor.

"Okay, I'm dazzled," Carlos said. "I can see it's time to bring out the big guns. This dance is called the Sorry, I Don't Have Any Spare Change, But I'll Be Happy to Use My Credit Card to Buy You a Sandwich."

It was a complicated dance. Carlos delivered a big shrug. He pulled his pockets inside out. He raised his index finger to signify an idea. He mimed pulling an imaginary credit card out of an imaginary wallet. He two-stepped over to an imaginary sandwich shop. He selected imaginary toppings. He accepted his imaginary sandwich. Then he performed a happy-skippy, this-is-a-yummy-sandwich jig.

It was an impressive performance, but it didn't impress everyone.

"STOP THAT TWITCHING!" Queen Cayenne screeched.

Everyone fell silent. Burly Guard stopped shouting. The music stopped playing. The miserable dancers stopped dancing miserably. Hortense stopped chewing his mini donuts. All eyes were on Carlos and Pinky.

"Oh, geez," Carlos mumbled.

"Meadows!" the queen said. "Please make a note that Prince Carlos of Faraway Kingdom is an idiot!"

"Yes, Your Majesty," Meadows replied.

CHAPTER 7

After the dancing came the party games.

"Meadows, please note that Princess Pinky is too sulky," the queen shouted.

"Yes, Your Majesty," Meadows replied. "Meadows, please note that Prince Carlos's smile looks forced and unconvincing."

"Yes, Your Majesty," Meadows replied.

"Meadows, please also note that both Prince Carlos and Princess Pinky are refusing to take a swing at the piñata shaped like King Carmine's head."

"Yes, Your Majesty," Meadows replied.

◆ ◆ ◆

After the party games came dinner.

"Meadows," the queen commanded, "please note that Prince Carlos dropped his salad spork on the floor!"

"Yes, Your Majesty," Meadows replied.

◆ ◆ ◆

Through it all, Hortense did nothing except sleepily eat sweets. He didn't play games or speak to anyone. He didn't even open his presents. That was the queen's job. She ripped off the wrapping paper and gave each gift a letter grade.

Hortense just kept eating. His mouth was ringed with a thick crust of frosting. His lap held a mountain of crumbs. Somehow he also got powdered sugar in his hair.

"Now, Hortense," the queen announced after the last package was open and graded, "it is time to give you *my* present."

The queen caressed her son's cheek (and tried her best to ignore the sticky goo that rubbed off onto her hand). "I have been the absolute ruler of Dire Dominion ever since your father was killed by a dragon. That was ten years ago today. They have been the happiest ten years of my life. There is nothing more wonderful than absolute power, son.

Nothing! So today, as my gift to you, I give you *power. My* power. *All* of it."

She let that sink in for a moment, then said, "From this moment forward, you are the absolute ruler of Dire Dominion!"

Carlos's mouth dropped open. "Queen Cayenne is giving absolute power to an eleven-year-old?" he whispered.

Pinky's mouth dropped open, too. "No," she replied, "Queen Cayenne is giving absolute power to a ten-and-three-quarters-year-old."

The queen spread her arms as wide as they could go. "This dominion is all yours, son," she exclaimed. "No need to thank me!"

Hortense didn't thank her. Instead, he poked another donut into his mouth.

"To claim your power, all you need to do is follow the ancient Dire Dominion tradition," she said. "On the day a new absolute ruler is selected, he or she *must* declare war."

The queen scanned her audience. She looked delighted by the dozens of terrified faces staring back at her.

"Choosing an enemy is not an easy decision, Hortense," she said, "so I'll help you out."

Burly Guard and Scarred Guard wheeled in a whiteboard. Scrawled upon it was a long list of names and numbers.

"Every kingdom on the continent is listed on this whiteboard," the queen said. "Next to each kingdom is a number. That number indicates how many times the kingdom attempted to ruin your birthday party. A few kingdoms listed here have a score of zero. That means they didn't ruin your party at all. These kingdoms respect Dire Dominion. These kingdoms respect *you*."

The queen leaned over to kiss her son's head but decided against it once she noticed all the powdered sugar. Straightening back up, she said, "Other kingdoms, however, do *not* respect you. The higher the number, the more that kingdom *hates* you."

All eyes fell upon the board. The king-doms were listed in ascending order. The lucky kingdoms, the zeros, were on the bottom. Most of the other kingdoms had scores in the single digits. The Democratic Republic of Dictatortot was third from the top with a score of thirteen.

Carlos was unable to catch his breath. Spot number two was Ever-After Land. And perched at the very top of the list, with a score of 592, was Faraway Kingdom.

How is that possible? Carlos thought. *I haven't even been here three hours! That's, like, three mistakes a minute!*

The queen smiled at Hortense. "All the evidence is before you, my wise son. It is now time to choose. Which kingdom shall we punish? Which kingdom will you destroy?"

King Hortense nodded. He licked his sticky fingers and wiped them on his silken robes, leaving long, chocolatey streaks behind.

King Hortense yawned. He yawned again. He rose from his throne and yawned a third time. Then he reached for another mini donut. Then he ate it. Slowly.

He turned his attention to the whiteboard. He carefully studied Faraway Kingdom's score.

It's going to happen, Carlos thought. *Dire Dominion is going to declare war on Faraway Kingdom.*

Carlos's stomach cramped in pain.

"As my first act as absolute ruler," Hortense began, "I will declare war on—"

But his last words were never spoken.

One of the ballroom's stained-glass windows exploded into a million pieces. Gray and brown shards scattered across the dance floor. Princes and princesses screamed. Guards lunged for their weapons. The queen's mouth dropped open. Hortense reached for another mini donut.

In the empty space where the window once stood was a large, angry horse.

"Cornelius," Carlos sighed. "I knew this day would come."

CHAPTER 8

Cornelius locked eyes with Carlos and charged.

Carlos reached for his sword. Before he could pull it from the scabbard, Cornelius was upon him. With his powerful head, Cornelius swatted the weapon from Carlos's grasp.

Cornelius swatted again, and Carlos flopped backward onto the floor.

Before he could get up, the horse planted his heavy front hooves on Carlos's shoulders. The boy was pinned to the floor.

Helpless.

"Wait!" Carlos protested. "Don't whole-body stub me!"

As Carlos spoke, he flailed around in search of a weapon.

Cornelius let out a victorious snort. Whole-body stubbing was *exactly* what the horse had in mind.

That's when Carlos felt a familiar object in his jacket's breast pocket.

Cornelius bared his teeth in a wicked smile.

Carlos fished the object from his pocket.

Cornelius attacked!

Carlos reached for Cornelius's face.

BZZZZ!

Carlos zapped Cornelius on the nose with his hand buzzer.

The startled horse flopped onto his butt. Carlos scrambled away, but Cornelius was soon hot on his heels.

Carlos put all his jester skills to use. He cartwheeled around the string quartet, somersaulted under the whiteboard, and leap-frogged over Meadows.

Cornelius had no jester skills, so he trampled the cello, snapped the whiteboard in half, and sent Meadows face-first into the punch bowl.

"Guards!" the queen wailed. "Stop that horse!"

But Cornelius could not be stopped. He

barreled toward the guards at a full gallop, knocking them down like a line of dominoes.

"Get out of here, Carlos!" Pinky yelled as she plunged a hand into her high hair. "I'll distract him!"

Pinky yanked a paintbrush from her updo. At once, her hair began to unravel.

She dipped the brush into a dollop of cake frosting and leapt into Cornelius's path.

The horse lunged, but Pinky sidestepped him and painted a frosting mustache on his upper lip.

"I call this move the Graffiti Artist," Pinky said with a smirk.

Cornelius launched a second attack. Pinky sidestepped that one, too, and turned the horse's mustache into a frosting goatee.

After Cornelius's third attack, Pinky brushed on a pair of goofy glasses.

By the time Pinky was through with him, Cornelius was painted up more than a mustachioed *Mona Lisa*.

Through it all, Queen Cayenne screamed.

"GUARDS!" she shouted.

But the guards were too dazed to respond.

"MEADOWS!" she shouted.

But Meadows was still blowing bubbles in the punch bowl.

"THE ARMY!" the queen shouted. "WHERE IS MY ARMY?"

But the army never arrived.

Carlos was running out of options. He wasn't fast enough or strong enough to out-run Cornelius for much longer. Carlos slid under a dinner table and hoped it would protect him.

It didn't. Cornelius kicked the table across the room. It slammed against a wall and broke into a thousand splinters.

Cornelius approached Carlos. His frosting mustache twitched in triumph.

Carlos closed his eyes and awaited his terrible fate.

Instead he heard a terrible noise.

It was Smudge crashing through a second stained-glass window!

"A DRAGON!" The queen fell backward in terror. "HELP!"

The princes and princesses screamed and scattered.

Smudge didn't seem to notice the ruckus. "Oh, hai, CC!" he said, gliding around the ballroom in a lazy circle. "I'm here to save you! Just like I said I would!"

"Smudge!" Carlos had never, ever been happier to see Smudge—and Carlos was *always* happy to see Smudge. "How did you get past those soldiers?"

"I knitted them wooly socks," Smudge said. "Soldier people really like toasty feet, CC!" The dragon thumped to the floor. He crinkled his eyebrows together. "Listen, horse. You're not gonna get my bestest friend all stubbed up!"

"GUARDS! DO SOMETHING! NOW!" The queen stumbled to her feet. Her hair was a mess and her dress was wrinkled. She also seemed a little dizzy. "KILL THAT DRAGON!"

The guards pulled themselves off the floor. Several of them reached for their swords. A few others reached for their

crossbows. They began to position themselves around the room.

Smudge counted the number of guards.
His eyes went wide with worry. "Six . . .
seven . . . eight people?" Smudge gulped. "And
a horse? This is not a fair fight, CC."

Cornelius turned to Smudge and gave
the dragon a hateful look. He scuffed the
dance floor with his front hoof like a bull
about to charge.

Smudge was going to be attacked, and
Carlos was powerless to stop it.

Or was he?

Carlos scanned the room. Resting by his

feet was the salad spork he had dropped at dinner.

He picked it up.

He remembered his new juggling routine. *Focus*, Carlos told himself. *Focus on the exact spot where you want the spork to land.*

Carlos closed his mind off to everything else. He focused.

With a quick snap of his elbow, Carlos threw the spork. It landed exactly where he wanted it to land.

Cornelius's rear end.

Carlos didn't know horses could scream. But they can. Cornelius leapt and bucked

and jumped and bellowed so loudly that Carlos had to cover his ears. The guards dropped their weapons and covered their ears, too.

Cornelius rampaged around the room. He smashed through yet another stained-glass window and galloped wildly toward the distant horizon.

Dang! Sporks are dangerous, Carlos thought. *I'd better come up with a new routine for the Stein triplets' birthday party.*

Queen Cayenne shook off her dizziness and surveyed the alarming sight. The ballroom was a disaster of shattered glass, mangled furniture, crumbling walls, and bruised guards.

She grabbed Hortense's jacket with one hand. With the other she pointed a bony, accusing finger at Carlos.

"He did this!" she wailed. "That wretched

Charming did *all* of this! Wage war on him!
Destroy that rotten Faraway Kingdom once
and for all!"

In reply, Hortense giggled.

The queen's eyes narrowed. "Are you giggling?"

Hortense giggled even more.

"Stop giggling!" The queen's voice grew low and menacing. "Wage war on Faraway Kingdom. NOW!"

But Hortense's giggle blossomed into a merry, wheezy laugh.

"I can't do that!" Hortense quivered with glee. "This was the most fun I've had in years! Did you see Prince Carlos buzz that horse's nose? Or the way he cartwheeled around the musicians?" He gasped for breath.

"ENOUGH OF THIS!" the queen roared so loudly that her voice made a fourth and final stained-glass window shatter. "If you're not going to declare war on Faraway Kingdom, then *I* will."

"You can't declare war," Pinky said. "Only the absolute ruler can declare war. You gave that power to Hortense!"

"That's right. You did," Carlos said. "I'm a witness."

"I'm a witness, too!" Smudge shouted.

"No, Smudge," Carlos said. "You didn't witness that."

"Oh, poop," Smudge replied.

"You may have your witnesses." The queen smiled. "But I have *the law*. And the law says you can't be the absolute ruler of Dire Dominion until you declare war!"

She folded her arms across her chest. "So!

The choice is yours, Hortense. Either declare war, or lose your power."

The room grew very still. Hortense bit his lower lip. He glanced at the battered whiteboard.

"Mom's right," Hortense sighed. "Dire Dominion will go to war whether I like it or not." He sighed again. "I just need to wage *one* war," he muttered to himself. "Just one. One war is not so bad. And then I can keep my power."

Hortense turned to the whiteboard again. He took a long, hard look at the second-highest number on the list of kingdoms. It was Ever-After Land. Pinky's kingdom.

Pinky clutched Carlos's hand. "Oh, no," she whispered.

Carlos whispered back, "Faraway Kingdom and Ever-After Land are best friends. If Dire Dominion wages war on you, we'll fight by your side."

Hortense cleared his throat. The guests held their breath.

"My first act as absolute ruler is to declare war on . . ." He paused. Then he smiled. "Boring parties!"

Everyone whooped and cheered.

Well, *almost* everyone.

"NOOOOO!" the queen sobbed. She stamped her feet and stormed from the room.

"You are a pretty good absolute ruler, Hortense," Carlos said.

"Thanks," Hortense replied. "So let's wage the war right now. Show me a few of those cool dance moves!"

"Awesome!" Carlos called out to the party guests. "Does anyone know how to play music that rocks?"

"On it!" Smudge announced. The dragon snapped up a flute and trilled out a power ballad.

The dancing began.

First, Carlos did the Empty the Dishwasher. Pinky followed it up with the I Really Shouldn't Have Eaten That Last Burrito.

Then Hortense tried a dance of his own called the Why, Yes, I Would Like Another Donut.

Before long, all the guests were going wild with dances of their own invention. Even Meadows and the dominion's guards busted a few moves.

It was a fantastic party.

After about a dozen songs, Pinky strutted to Carlos's side. "Hey. Wanna shake things up with a box step?" she asked.

Carlos kind of did. "Okay," he said.

He took Pinky's hand. Moments later, the two of them were counting off steps.

"Hortense hasn't stopped laughing for the last hour," Pinky said. "I think Dire Dominion is out of the war business once and for all."

Carlos's eyes sparkled.

"What is it?" Pinky asked.

"You just reminded me of something," Carlos replied. "A long time ago, in the early days of my training, Jack the Jester told me something."

"What did he say?"

"He said, 'A laughing world is a happier world. A more peaceful world. A jolly, jelly-belly, silly world!'"

Carlos smiled at the memory.

"It looks like you proved him right," Pinky said.

Carlos shook his head. "We *both* proved him right."

Pinky didn't reply to that. She just smiled a little and looked down at her feet.

Carlos did the same.

He watched his own scuffed boots and Pinky's muddy, bare feet move in perfect sync.

Forward. Side. Together.

Backward. Side. Together.

ABOUT THE AUTHOR

Roy L. Hinuss is the authorized biographer of the Charming Royal Family. He is also fond of the occasional fart joke. When he isn't writing about Prince Carlos Charles Charming's many adventures, he serves as the president of PITCH-SPORK, an anti-spork lobbying organization. Be sure to sign the petition on Facebook!

**Don't miss any of
the adventures in the
Prince Not-So Charming series!**

PRINCE NOT-SO CHARMING
Once Upon a Prank
Roy L. Hinuss

PRINCE NOT-SO CHARMING
Her Royal Slyness
Roy L. Hinuss

PRINCE NOT-SO CHARMING
The Dork Knight
Roy L. Hinuss